Spacers Snarled in the Hair of Comets

Bruce Boston

Introduction:
Andrew Darlington

Mind's Eye Publications

Poems in this collection have appeared, sometimes in slightly different form, in the following publications: *Aboriginal SF, Aliens and Lovers, Amazing Stories, Asimov's SF Magazine, Contemporary Rhyme, DreamForge, Eotu, Eye to the Telescope, Fantasy Commentator, The Magazine of Speculative Poetry, Mythic Delirium, Poly: New Speculative Writing, Science Fiction Age, Star*Line, Talebones, and Velocities.*

First Edition 2022
ISBN-13: 978-1-7367114-4-6
ISBN-10: 1-7367114-4-6

Cover Collage: Bruce Boston, for
the poem, "Dark Rains Here and There"

Introduction
by Andrew Darlington

Book Design: Bruce Boston & Frank Coffman

Mind's Eye Publications
mindseye.us.com

Contents

The Outward Urge

Boston shapes unlikely geometries that cast tall shadows. With internal rhymes that spring sudden trapdoors of pleasure, and where phrases return like relentless assassins. Where innovation and continuity are caught up by the gravity waves of new equations. Here are thaumaturgical star-spark mythologies in the guise of old legends for new Earths, meetings beyond infinity, before they run out of sky.

Was there Science Fiction before there was science? There were always epic voyages that spawned fantastic tales of heroic adventure. That's a human constant. The poem "Song Of The Eternal Sailors" is the alchemic key to unlock its secrets, misguiding enchanted voyagers back to Homer, with Odysseus outwitting the Cyclops while lured by the deadly song of Sirens, I know – I've been to Ithaca, I've walked that same shingle. There were sailors on the seas of fate back before the world was round, questing with peg-legged Ahab, pursuing truths that can never be snared, as Jules Verne's 'Nautilus' glides the green dimension beneath the event horizon of the sea. John Wyndham termed it 'the outward urge'. The restless drive that took proto-humans around the globe, that will propel future star-sailors across the Magellanic Cloud blown on solar winds. And this one comes within the soft flow of a rhyme-scheme.

Bruce Boston was born in Chicago, irradiated by San-Fran psychedelics and Cold War strontium-90 fall-out, but he works off-planet. He has a Spacer's soul. The title-poem of this collection won the 1985 'Rhysling Award For Speculative Poetry'... but that was simply one of seven poems to achieve that distinction. One of many honours and awards deservedly heaped on his shoulders. Here there be more sensuous debris, more songs of the stars, songs of the dark... one poem – called "The Poetry Of Science Fiction", is made up of book and magazine titles. See how many you can identify, while you fill your pockets with stars. Another charts a hundred years of dreaming for the hibernating crew of an outbound starship, for 'imagination's journeys are of a different brand.' Boston coins new phrases in alien currencies.

This book is a thousand-year diary. And also a rehearsal for disaster. The Folk-music of tomorrow, even if there is no tomorrow. Fables and cybertexts, hypertales and metafictions of violent worlds where the big bang either never happened, or is caught in a repetition of renewing primal detonations. Lost in the freezing emptiness between worlds where light crawls to a halt on the rim of eternity, a cold mathematics of the unimaginable possibilities that Boston fills with beguiling organisms across the spattered galactic oceans aswim with cetacean suns and cockleshell planets. These are tall tales romanced and retold in the brawling taverns of Mars or the dim café's of Aldebaran, in the backstreets of starport cities, beneath the light of alien suns, where scientists research and experiment with no conception of the awesome forces they dice with, in printouts that burn with the incendiary frequencies of sine-wave modulations.

Space has no directions, yet holds all directions in itself. An eternal throb. New tales for bright dreamings. Meet Bruce Boston in the shades of forever.

Andrew Darlington
West Yorkshire, England
January 2022

*Spacers Snarled
in the Hair Of Comets*

For Spacers Snarled in the Hair of Comets

If you've heard the stellar *vox humana*
the untuned ear takes for static,

if you've kissed the burning eyelids
of god and seized upon the moon's

reflection, disjointed and backwards,
in the choppy ink of some alien sea,

then you know how sleek and fleshy,
how treacherous, the stars can become.

While the universe falls with no boundary,
you and I sit in a cafe of a port city

on a planet whose name we've forgotten:
the vacuum is behind us and before us,

the spiced ale is cool and hallucinogenic.
Already the candle sparkles in our plates.

A Spacer's Life Is Ice and Fire

Inward along the speckled arm
of our turning spiral nebula
I FTL-ed it in whatever ship
would gain me ready passage,
so raw and green at first
until the burning darkness
laced my spacer's boots.

Inward through parsecs
of always changing light
and chill blue slumber,
awakening on worlds
where sense or passion
claimed my heady flight,
yet only in the passing.
So very green at first
until the rush of night
claimed my spacer's soul.

Inward to the epicenter
of our churning star swarm
where thoughts ineffable
could flourish and bloom,
where the universal light
at the galactic core
could fuse my sight
with visions quintessential,
with rich illuminations

beyond what's understood.

Burning green to metagreen,
a rush of colors in between.
Mandalic moons, sidereal seas.
A spacer's life is ice and fire,
graced by iridescent dreams.

The Eyes of the Pilot

The breath of many worlds
sifting through her blood,
a wealth of alien images
overflowing the faceted orbs
of her mind's projection,
she shapes unlikely geometries
of spatial condensation
and leaps unerringly
on the template of the stars.

Here she is alone in the dark
and stretched very thin,
four thousand tons of steel
and flesh trailing behind,
patterned and at one
with the universal birth
of stellar excitation.

Here the Doppler fractions,
and each line of thought
that clicks smoothly
in the breach of acceleration,
instantly threads
the shifting parameters
of force and inclination.

Always the light returns
like a relentless assassin,

the attenuated atoms assemble
and she unclips the sensors
to breathe again: her thought
once more is only thought,
her eyes, blue cognizance
fixed in transient space,
reflect her destination.

The Veracity of Imagination

Impossible...they once said!
Nothing moves faster than light.
It's beyond the constraints
of the space/time continuum.
Yet now we do it every day!
Blood and sweat and calculation

sends these behemoths flickering
through the interstellar dark
to emerge beside a farther star.
Human desperation/aspiration
to transcend the static moment,
to deliver any given reality

our FTL-minds can comprehend:
this is the force that drives
our being through the night
and folds the fabric of space.
And as the planes of the plenum
open to us, one way or a dozen,

open like the palm of a hand,
like a wound, like the wings
of the gigantic lepidopteron
of Fretas IV as it first senses
the rays of its blue-white sun,
the unconstrained universe

will be splayed and revealed.
Impossible...they always say,
as they have learned to say.
Meet me in shades of tomorrow!
And remember, we are forever
touching the body of space.

Song of the Eternal Sailors

From Liverpool to Shanghai, the waterways we roam.
The wave roar and the salt spray are our only home.
Across the dark Sargasso, into the chilling winds,
The wages of the past have covered all our sins.

Old Chorus:
Ah the sea so bright and eager,
O the ocean dark and wide,
Let the waters answer for us all.

Odysseus was the captain as we rowed across the waves.
We left the Cyclops blinded in the hollow of his caves.
We saw the singing Sirens, we could not hear their call,
Their beauty like a burning brand upon us one and all.

We sailed to the ocean's edge before the earth was round,
The flapping of the sails made such a mournful sound.
Like men without a country, but for the country blue.
The maps are ever changing, the shoals are always new.

We rode with peglegged Ahab and how the man did rave.
His wooden limb is floating in the waters of his grave.
We scanned that thin horizon for a plume against the sky,
And when we manned the longboats, we let the steel fly.

With Nemo on the Nautilus we moved beneath the seas,
Alive under a rippling sky, with seaweed for our trees.
At forty fathoms down below, the silence reigns supreme.

The streets we left behind exist as no more than a dream.

Now we've fled the mother world and sailed into space,
As misfits, outcasts, pioneers...of the human race.
Across the Magellanic Clouds, propelled by solar winds,
The wages of the past have covered all our sins.

New Chorus:
Ah the stars so bright and eager,
O the light years dark and wide,
Let the vacuum answer for us all.

The Ice Miners

In the rush and pull
of asynchronous orbits,
in helmeted and suited suspension,
we tap the well of space
and are gone
with the swimming light.

We fall sunward,
yet even with the great
lasered disks of ice in tow
our shifting umbra
is but a speck
on the gutted shell of Callisto.

Our near weightless journey
is as tedious as
the silence we traverse.

Yet everywhere our caravans have passed,
from the bumpy free-floating
geodesic of New Chicago
to the boom towns of Mars,
we have become the stuff of legend.

Water-bearers.
Nomads and life-givers.
Through the desert of the stellar night.

The Mating of the Storm Birds

When the storm birds cry and rise,
their great wingspans
white against the violet day,
or dark upon the stars,
we know the wind and rain
lie soon behind.

Safe within our metal hulls
for weeks at a time
we hear their fierce ecstatic
krees! as they ride the gusts,
their song a descant
within the storm's dense pounding.

Afterward it is silent
but for the drip and pool of water.
The red sun returns to the violet sky,
and here and there across the muddied landscape
we find them: feathers smudged,
huge beaks slack, bones twisted
like the struts of broken gliders.
Their eyes, close on the moment of death,
still shine with a luminous intensity.

Across the valley in the nesting cliffs
fledglings hop awkwardly
up and down the dark escarpments.
They will wait through a year
of slowly changing seasons
for their own moments
of grace and joyous expiration.

The Music of Deep Spacers

From the brawling bars of Mars
to the dim cafes of Aldebaran,
the music of deep spacers

reaches to the unbounded sky.
Most often it is a raucous music
of passions intense and fleeting,

brutal and lacking in subtlety,
a release from light years passed.
Yet when the last call comes and

the lights flicker, and cafes
and dim bars are shutting down,
the music all at once changes

to a vast and haunting refrain
that echoes the depths of space,
the solitude of ceaseless travel.

Stumbling out into the night,
singly, in pairs, and in groups,
strains of music trailing behind,

the spacers wander alien streets,
in search of temporary lodgings
beneath the static of the stars.

Beyond the Edge of Alien Desire

Seduced by pheromones
more potent to the senses
then my species' own,
I ride her blue cries
to crimson excitations,
and for a trembling instant
the light years between
our limbs collapse.

Charged by the tendrils
of her spiked electric fur
to telepathic sight,
I feel pain raining down,
see blue fields blown
in the searing light,
know the wiles of victims
for the pale glabrous beasts
who handle them by night.

At dawn the dreadnaughts leap,
another world to take,
her scent is still upon me,
blue miles to go before I wake.

The Star Dreamers

They froze us instantaneously
for our journey to far stars.
They stacked us tier on tier
in the darkness of the hold.
While generations passed
on the world we left behind
we would age a single day
and know a senseless night,
and then we would awaken
with our youth still at hand.

They said we would not dream,
but oh they were so wrong.
We dreamed a thousand dreams
in a hundred years of sleep.
We lived without existing
in the landscapes of our minds,
while the silent parsecs passed
and our starship traveled on
to find some world to conquer
where new life could abound.

At last our coffins cracked
and our wintry eyelids thawed.
Our bodies slowly warmed
yet our brains still held a chill.
Our mirrors reflected youth,
unblemished and pristine,

but mirrors can surely lie:
We were wrinkled deep within.
Far more than supple limbs,
youth dwells within the mind.

Now that we've awakened
to confront a waiting world,
we balk at the adventure,
we have spent the urge to try.
We have dreamt so many lives
that our appetite for life
has lost its cutting edge and
been ground down by time.
Dreams are less than real
yet their sum can fill the years.

Beneath a distant saffron sun
that will offer little heat,
we let the steam from our cups
rise against our downy cheeks.
If we plan to survive there
are tasks we should define.
Instead we sit and barter
tales of lives we never lived,
of worlds we never conquered
and things we never did.

The Dimensional Rush of Relative Primes

When Theda slipped into
a life of leisure
on eleven planets,
she had no idea of
the alien opportunities
she would endure.

At the end of her
journey lay the instant
known as Earth.
Teeming as it was,
she remained human
among others as such.

She missed the sure
exaltations that stellar
realms had to offer,
the swift acceleration
and dimensional rush
of relative primes.

Most of all the slender
tripeds of Nine-Four-Three,
intimate in their bravura.

Someday she would teach
her children's children
about the wages of space,

how in traveling from
one world to another
you are transubstantiated.

In that telling she would
conjugate the rules
of her digression
and the subsequent
definition of a self
she could not deny.

Illuminating her past and
its brash indiscretions,
she would prove without
the sun of a doubt
that the stars are fire.

The Star Drifter Grounded

In the back streets of a starport city
the drifter waits out the short years
with assorted otherworldly cronies
and an occasional native concubine.

Circling too close for comfort
to a brilliant white dwarf,
sweltering beneath the cloud-clotted skies,
the drifter waits out the short years,
no longer bothering with conversions.

The natives here are blue-skinned
and angular, yet they are humanoid,
soft in the right places,
as graceful as the saplings of
...but he can no longer recall
the name of that planet.

Each day he crosses the muggy streets
to read the notices on a union board:
Europa, Class AA tonnage, Earth Registry,
inbound for Sol by way of Bryan's Star,
WANTED: one mate, two mechs, one 'gator.

His skills are many, his papers in order,
but they tell him he is too old
for the rigors of stardrive,
too old to ride the spokes of light
like fire in his thighs,

too old to brave the vacuum.

\#

Zenthyl, his friend from Nuvie IV,
claims that any land is lovable.
Take a steady mate, Zenthyl counsels,
forget the foolishness of star lust.
Yet Zenthyl's skin does not rot
in the damp of this greenhouse world.

So he works the docks
and saves what money he can,
handling crates hammered under other skies,
the stuff of alien worlds
passing beneath his calloused hands.

On the dark slate walls of his hut,
with a stub of chalk,
while curious children watch
and others shake their heads
at the inscriptions of a madman,
he draws the constellations
he can no longer see.

Where to go? — where to go? —
once he has saved the passage.
His only home
the emptiness between worlds,
gravity free he dreams the stars,
the tachyon drive spitting at his back,

the singing fission.

#

Drinking in a spacer's bar is costly,
so some nights he drinks alone.
And when he has had his fill
he staggers into the tepid night,
bare to the waist, his belly
gray-haired and round as a pot,
still hard beneath the aging flesh.

His eyes and thoughts are empty.
There is an incandescence in his heart,
a wilderness of light; above there is
nothing but a vague gray blackness.

If only he could see the stars:
giant red Betelgeuse,
bright Procyon with its host of planets,
Alcor and Mizar in their flaming binary dance.
But those are only names,
and beyond the closely packed cloud cover
he can no longer be sure they remain.

In a score of short years
he will heed wise Zenthyl's advice.
He will take a steady blue woman.
Instead of stars he will dream
the impossible child
of their impossible union.

The FTL Addict Fixes

Beyond the system's fall,
upon a hill in empty space,
my mind recalls
in spokes upon the sky
the glint of colors newly named.

My mind recalls
the taste of patterns raw,
of bone and blood
and matted thought as one.

In pale resolution
cabin walls shimmer and flee,
and I am nailed free
to the struts of a flailing universe,
specked to each bald star.

A being and nothingness
on the tense of time.

Come faster sweet steel,
give me your light sinews,
your latticed and crystalline flower,
the abstract particulars of your death speed.

Beneath an Alien Sky

43 light years from Earth
the native constellations
of another world
pass across the sky.

When the moon rises
from the Western Sea,
Shavrr, The Thief, flees
to the darker East.

The Exalted Mage Sste-Lan,
his long hair riding
a trail of stars,
follows close behind.

Jav, the six-legged beast,
takes the pole position,
his leathery trunk arching
in a parabola of light.

In the relativity
of space and time,
Earth remains invisible
as the farthest stars.

Yet still the sidereal
shapes of night remain,
arbitrary and bright
as any work of art.

Curse of the Star-Pilot's Husband

In the vast envelope of stellar space
she has conjugated every constellation
and calculated instantaneous interstellar
trajectories that convert the inconceivable
distances of the space-time continuum
to the flip of a switch, a single calibration.

She has sampled systems by the score,
planets and moons by a score times ten,
the colors and vistas of alien landscapes,
the incomprehensible customs of complex
extraterrestrial cultures, the flavors and
fashions of worlds far beyond human ken.

When he kamasutras her from head to toe
with tactile skill (even if he does it twice),
when he exhibits the long-distance stamina
of a marathon medalist and explores every
erogenous nook and cranny known to man,
she merely whispers: "That was nice."

In Praise of Timelessness

Hours and minutes have fled.
Seconds are as elusive as ever.
There are no right years anymore.
No true decades or centuries.

As the climes of humankind
resonate through the universe
the rules of relative space
takes on absolute significance

and each meandering soul must
cast its own clock and calendar.
Like the dust from entropic stars
generations drift and coalesce,

epochs intertwine, styles abound
until all times are in fashion,
abetted by the lightning miles,
red-shifted in constant revision.

Even those sacred nigh-immortals
who now travel openly among us
(envied by some, pitied by others),
their scattered faces baldly aglow

with the luminous high senility
of their wasted age and wisdom,
brain-frayed and bare sensual

as only the brain-frayed can be,

must tread each ripening instant
as if it were the first and last.
As we all are compelled to begin
again in this age of strayed color

and chronological calculation.
Shedding our outdated histories
like the husks of dry chrysali,
watching the past obliterate,

we are birthed to transience.
We learn to inhabit and embrace
the staggered synchronicity
of algorithmic space.

In a Spacers' Bar

I met him in a spacers' bar,
spacers jostling side by side,
intoxicants of every brand,
legal and the other kind.

Flesh as tan as seasoned brick.
His face was old and wise.
Hair a shock of blazing white.
His presence burned like ice.

He told me of his journeys
far across galactic space,
to worlds I'd only heard about,
worlds I never knew were there.

He'd seen the Arthropod Alliance
that dominates the Milky Core,
the splendors of their Architects,
the rampant fury of their Lords.

He'd piloted the Border Worlds
on the fringe of starless black,
where outlaw spacers go to die
with dreams of coming back.

He'd fought in wars aplenty
that had known no real source,
beyond some tyrant's dream

to commandeer the universe.

And the suffering he'd seen
weighed on him like a star,
that flared behind his eyes
with a rage of ice and fire.

Then I talked to other spacers
and two aliens from Tzara,
who claimed he was a lunatic
who had never left the Earth,

a deranged cost accountant
who dreamed a spacer's berth.
But then again, I thought,
in a way he really had,

for imagination's journeys
are of a different brand.
And the stories that he told
were wine fresh from the vine,

raw in flavor, rich with life,
ablaze within my mind,
far more full of fire and ice
than anything of mine.

A Spacer's Tale

Bound by the pull of gravity
where lives and empires fail,
on a planet rife with savagery,
where sticks and stones prevail,

you may awaken to a certainty
that is like no other kind,
the force of its symmetry
sounding through your mind.

All of you and all of me
and others far from fine,
can polish stones to entropy
and even make them shine.

Beyond the pull of gravity
where imagination sails,
on a planet rich in majesty,
you can live a spacer's tale.

Dark Rains Here and There

i

When she was a girl in Myanmar
the dark rains fell
suddenly in great sheets
of water and sound
in the heated afternoons.

Thunder would rattle
the tin roof and the kitchen
would often flood.

When the dark rains fell on Myanmar
she lived in poverty beneath
the tyranny of a state
beyond redemption.

When the dark rains fell on Myanmar
the sky gave up its color.
Shadows would disappear
for there would be one great shadow
covering everything.

ii

When she was a woman in San Francisco
the dark rains would fall slowly
and steadily for days at a time,

turning the pastel houses gray
beneath an even grayer sky.

When the dark rains fell on San Francisco
the tires of passing cars hissed
endlessly on the wet pavements.

When the dark rains fell on San Francisco
she lived with passion and belief
and drug-fueled flights to worlds unfathomed.

iii

When she was a wanderer in space,
the dark rains fell many ways
on many different worlds.

When the dark rains fell
in the labyrinth of canyons
that laced the southern hemisphere
of Epsilon Eridani Nine,
they danced this way and that
in constantly shifting whirlpools of wind.

When the dark rains fell in the light gravity
of Fomalhaut's only habitable moon,
it was in large limpid drops
clinging to the cilia and limbs
of overarching trees.

When the dark rains fell

on many different worlds,
here and there,
she learned to live with love
bright as a rocket's flare
and loss deep as a singularity.

iv

When she was a señora
in the high Mexico desert,
in the steady days
of her peace and resolution,
she would stand at the screen door
just before dusk.

She would listen to the insects ticking
against the dusty metal crosshatch
and watch the light
from a low red sun
encroaching on the shade of the porch.

When the sky remained cloudless
on the high desert,
when life seemed dry and spare
as the land around her,
she found herself watching
for one more dark rain
she could walk in.

Interstellar Tract

after William Carlos Williams

I will teach you my Earth people
how to perform a star flight
for you have it over a troop
of astronauts –
you have the space sense necessary.

See! imagination leads.
I begin with a design for a ship.
For Sol's sake not streamlined –
not silver either – and not polished!
Let it be weathered and familiar,
as full of natural color
as the world it leaves behind.

And let us have glass on all sides!
Yes windows, my Earth people!
To what purpose? So we might
see the stars streak in the wake
of our light-speed passage,
so we might watch our past shrink
and our future swell before us.

No plastics please –
and if there must be steel
for Clarke's sake keep it covered.
Fill the corridors with earth
which gives beneath our feet,

where grass can begin to grow.
Plaster the walls and panels
with murals of your own making
or common mementos from the past,
a favorite poem or photograph –
an old poster – a dried flower –
you know the things I mean
my Earth people.

Better still, no corridors at all,
no cramped cabins to hold us in –
rather a vast and open space,
spun for gravity, where our
thoughts may freely flow,
with a river known for its warmth,
a forest or two so we can build
homes of our own choice.

A rough and natural ship then,
a miniature Earth, still clean –
green and blue and full of clouds
if you can imagine such a thing –
and for light no glowing tubes
that turn the skin a sickly hue,
but the passing stars themselves –
magnified by sufficient art and craft
to rival the lumens of our sun.

As for the bridge and crew –
bring them down – bring them down!
A navigator, perhaps, to help

plot our course between systems,
but no communications officer
to turn our varied voices into one,
no strutting captain-king
leading us through the cosmos,
calling our ship his ship.

Let the controls remain simple.
For what reason? So any man
or woman can learn to master them,
so every one of us might take a turn
at the board and have a hand
in making our destinations.

And finally, each sidereal cycle,
let us sit openly with one another,
side by side beneath the trees –
my Earth people – as we conspire
to save the best in our origins
and leave the worst behind –
you have nothing to lose –
believe me, the stars
will fill your pockets.

Go ahead now –
I think you are ready for flight.

The Poetry of Science Fiction*

Against the fall of night,
across the wounded galaxies,
envoy to new worlds,
behold the man –he, she, and it!–
born into light, dying of the light,
becoming alien between worlds,
a new species more than human
always coming home
alone against tomorrow.

Time and again, those who can,
change the sky and all between.
We cast down the stars,
four hundred billion stars
on wings of song.
Brightness falls from the air,
downward to the Earth,
down the bright way
burning with a vision.
Earth abides, a swiftly tilting
planet in the ocean of night.

Explorers of the infinite,
exiled from Earth,
dancing at the edge of the world,
we call back yesterday
in memory yet green.
We return to Earth

but we are not of the Earth.
The future took us out there
across the sea of suns
in search of forever,
beyond the blue event horizon
where time winds blow.

Lest darkness fall
you shall know them.
Strange relations. Strange
ports of call. Strange horizons
from utopia to nightmare.
Star-line velocities ten thousand
light years from home.
Men like gods. Women of wonder
holding your eight hands.
The shape of things to come.

The stars are ours – take back plenty!
Dream the creation of tomorrow!
Dream the last dangerous visions!

—

*This poem is composed entirely from the
titles of science fiction books and periodicals.

Spacer's Compass

South I shipped…galactic south
spanning the reaches of unbounded space
    through the moss stars and beyond
hanging with this crew or that
      a rough lot they were
      or some just strange
  stranger than you'd care to know
    for a light year or two on the fly

West I wandered…galactic west
      leaving lovers changing friends
   past clusters hanging in the heavens
    like burning ingots and bands of flame
landing always in a different land
     a ready cup for alien ways
      seeking never so much an answer
as a fix…a frame of reference
    to sift my strangeness from

East I flew…galactic east
  against the words of wiser souls
    to decaying grandeurs steeped in fog
      and cultures deadly spent
    to language worlds and pleasure worlds
  and the mother world or fabled so
     a desolation of rust and snow
       heir only to its past

Old I grow…galactic old
 the polar night now calls my name
  and still I tramp the stellar routes
   from burning white to burning red
    jump cutting lives and lands
   fixing no frame of reference
    beyond the passage itself
     adrift in the passages
      yet to be taken

  Space has no directions
   and holds all directions at once
    a well of radiant possibilities
   all matter of strangeness

    …and the stars are for the living

Bruce Boston is the author of sixty books and chapbooks, including the novels *Stained Glass Rain* and *The Guardener's Tale*. His poems and stories have appeared in hundreds of publications, most visibly in *Analog, Asimov's SF, Amazing Stories, Weird Tales, New Myths, Strange Horizons, The Pedestal Magazine, Daily Science Fiction, Year's Best Horror* (DAW), *Year's Best Fantasy and Horror* (St. Martin's), *and the Nebula Awards* Showcase (St. Martin's), and received numerous awards, most notably the Bram Stoker Award, a Pushcart Prize, the *Asimov's* Readers Award, and the Rhysling and Grand Master Awards of the SFPA.

http://www.bruceboston.com
http://www.facebook.com/bruce.boston.50

Andrew Darlington watched the very first episode of *Dr Who*. He also watched the most recent episode. Whatever academic potential he may once have possessed was wrecked by an addiction to loud Rock 'n' Roll and cheap Science Fiction, which remain the twin poles of what he laughingly refers to as his writing career. He is most proud of his Parallel Universe collection "A Saucerful Of Secrets". His latest books include a biography of the Beatles' spin-doctor *Derek Taylor: For Your Radioactive Children*, and *On Track: The Hollies, Every Album, Every Song* (both from SonicBond Books). His writing can be found at "Eight Miles Higher":

http://andrewdarlington.blogspot.co.uk/

Fiction by Bruce Boston

The Guardener's Tale

"A gripping dystopia wickedly extrapolated from our present. Boston brings to bear his narrative genius on this noir tale of a love triangle in a society gone mad, probing the way technology and science alter our reality. Transcending genre, *The Guardener's Tale* combines suspense and breathtaking plot twists with macabre humor. Involving, compelling, a masterwork."
—Mary Turzillo, Nebula Award author of *An Old-Fashioned Martian Girl*

Bram Stoker Award Finalist, trade paper and ebook, 273 pages

Masque of Dreams

"One of Wildside's latest comes from poet Bruce Boston, whose prose sings like a mix of E.T.A. Hoffman and Hawthorne, Borges and Bierce. His *Masque of Dreams* collects nearly two dozen brilliant stories, ranging across all emotional and narrative terrains."
– Paul Di Filippo, *The Washington Post*

"...a great talent for richly evoking a place in time...a gift for creating memorable characters.... The stories and poems have in common Boston's well-trained poet's eye for detail, his beautifully crafted language, and his unfailing compassion for his characters...sure to leave readers dazzled by the depth and range of his talents." – Tim Pratt, *Locus*

Best-Of Story Collection, hard cover and trade paper, 297 pages

Available from Amazon
and other online booksellers.

More from Mind's Eye Publications

SPECULATIONS:
Poetry from the Weird Poets Society Facebook Group from 2018 vol. 1, 2019

SPECULATIONS II:
Poetry from the Weird Poets Society Facebook Group from 2019 vol. 2 — 2020

SPECULATIONS II:
Poetry from the Weird Poets Society Facebook Group from 2020 vol. 3 — 2021

The Exorcised Lyric
Poems by Steven Withrow & Frank Coffman
Cover & Illustrations by Mutartis Boswell 2021

Eclipse of the Moon
Frank Coffman's third major collection of speculative verse Cover & Illustrations by Mutartis Boswell 2021

Three Against the Dark:
Collected Dr. Venn Occult Detective Mysteries
By Frank Coffman
Cover & Illustrations by Yves Tourigny 2022